MO
and His Friends

MARY POPE OSBORNE

PICTURES BY

DyAnne DiSalvo-Ryan

PUFFIN BOOKS

For Ken Whelan, the real Mo
—*M.P.O.*

For Vanessa and Michael Jo
—*D.D.*

PUFFIN BOOKS
Published by the Penguin Group
Penguin Books USA Inc., 375 Hudson Street, New York, New York 10014, U.S.A.
Penguin Books Ltd, 27 Wrights Lane, London W8 5TZ, England
Penguin Books Australia Ltd, Ringwood, Victoria, Australia
Penguin Books Canada Ltd, 10 Alcorn Avenue, Toronto, Ontario, Canada M4V 3B2
Penguin Books (N.Z.) Ltd, 182-190 Wairau Road, Auckland 10, New Zealand

Penguin Books Ltd, Registered Offices: Harmondsworth, Middlesex, England

First published in the United States of America by Dial,
a division of Penguin Books USA Inc., 1989
Published simultaneously in Canada by Fitzhenry & Whiteside, Limited, Toronto
Published in a Puffin Easy-to-Read edition, 1996

1 3 5 7 9 10 8 6 4 2

Text copyright © Mary Pope Osborne, 1989
Illustrations copyright © DyAnne DiSalvo-Ryan, 1989
All rights reserved

THE LIBRARY OF CONGRESS HAS CATALOGED THE DIAL EDITION AS FOLLOWS:
Osborne, Mary Pope. Mo and his friends / by Mary Pope Osborne;
pictures by DyAnne DiSalvo-Ryan.
p. cm.
Summary: Brief stories feature Sheriff Mo and his animal friends.
ISBN 0-8037-0504-2. ISBN 0-8037-0505-0 (lib. bdg.)
[1. Friendship—Fiction. 2. Animals—Fiction.]
I. DiSalvo-Ryan, DyAnne, ill. II. Title.
PZ7.081167Mm 1989   [E]—dc19   87-15655   CIP   AC

Puffin Books ISBN 0-14-036202-9

Puffin® and Easy-to-Read® are registered trademarks of Penguin Books USA Inc.
Printed in the United States of America

Reading Level 2.1

Contents

AUNT MINNIE TAKES A BREAK

Aunt Minnie worked very hard
in her boardinghouse
beside Smith Pond.
She cooked and swept.
She washed clothes
and fixed broken steps.

"Aunt Minnie needs a break,"

Peewee said.

"She certainly does!" said Pearl.

"Let's give her a vacation."

"Good idea," said Peewee.

So Pearl and Peewee had a bake sale

and a car wash to raise money

for Aunt Minnie's vacation.

Then they had a party

for Aunt Minnie.

"Aunt Minnie, here's fifty dollars!"

Pearl said.

"For a vacation in Florida!"

Aunt Minnie clapped her hands.

"You are so nice to do this!" she said.

Chicken Lucille helped Aunt Minnie
pack for her trip.
Then Peewee bought her a bus ticket.

The night before Aunt Minnie left,

Sheriff Mo heard a knock on his door.

"Aunt Minnie! Come in!

Sit down!" he said. "How are you?"

"Oh, Sheriff," Aunt Minnie said.

"I don't want to go away!"

She burst into a flood of tears.

"I'll be just miserable

without all my friends."

"Oh, I see, I see," said Mo,

patting her on the back.

"Well, don't worry, Aunt Minnie.

I'll think of something."

The next morning everyone took
Aunt Minnie to the bus station.
"Where's Sheriff Mo?" asked Aunt Minnie.
"He said he would meet us here,"
said Chicken Lucille.

Just then the bus pulled up.

"Oh, dear, oh, dear," said Aunt Minnie.

"We must wait for the sheriff!"

"We'll tell Mo you said good-bye,"

said Pearl. "It's time to go now."

Just then the door to the bus opened.

"All aboard!" shouted Sheriff Mo.

Mo was the bus driver!

"We are all going on a trip!" he said.

"Together!"

Then Mo drove everyone to the beach.

For three days they had a great time.

Peewee took pictures

as they built sandcastles,

and Sheriff Mo read

under a striped umbrella.

Then they all came back home,
sunburned and happy.
And Aunt Minnie stayed up all night
sweeping sand out of the bus.

THE QUEEN BY THE POND

One day Pearl and Peewee spied

a strange creature

strolling around Smith Pond.

She appeared to be a queen.

She wore a gold crown on her head
and a long purple cape.
And she had on a white mask
and waved a large flowered fan.
"*Who* is that?" said Peewee.
"Oh, dear! I don't know!" said Pearl.

The two of them ran to Sheriff Mo's.

"Hurry, Sheriff!" they cried.

"A strange creature who looks like

a queen is walking around the pond!"

"Goodness," said Mo.

And he rushed to the pond

with Pearl and Peewee.

Now many other animals were watching the queen in the white mask strolling about, waving her fan.

"Excuse me, madame," said Mo.

"But what are you doing here?"

"Enjoying your lovely sun, Sheriff," said the queen in a high voice.

"Who are you?" asked Mo.

"You may call me Queen Blanche," the queen said sweetly.

"Ah!" said Mo.

He recognized a familiar voice.

"I have an idea, madame," he said.

Everyone watched as Mo got
some boards and a hammer and nails,
and made a little platform.
Then he put up a curtain.

"From now on everyone can come here
to see plays!" he said.

"What plays?" asked Pearl.

"Plays starring Chicken Lucille!"
Mo said.

Later Chicken Lucille said to Mo,
"My dream of being an actress
has finally come true, thanks to you."
"You deserve it, Lucille," said Mo
as everyone applauded.

PEEWEE'S SURPRISE

Early one autumn morning

Chicken Lucille, Aunt Minnie, and Mo

knocked on Peewee's door.

"I'm coming," called Peewee.

He took a large sack from his closet.

Then he left the house with
Aunt Minnie, Mo, and Chicken Lucille.
They tramped into the woods
and picked nuts and acorns
off the ground.

They picked apples

off the apple trees

and berries off the berry bushes

and put them into Peewee's sack.

Then they walked beside a stream.

And near the water

Aunt Minnie found a blue stone.

Chicken Lucille found a pink stone.

They put them both in Peewee's sack.

Then Peewee climbed a maple tree
and pulled red leaves
off the branches.

And Mo picked purple clover,
wild daisies, and buttercups.
They put them all in Peewee's sack.

Then Sheriff Mo, Aunt Minnie,
Chicken Lucille, and Peewee
went to Pearl's house.

Inside, Pearl was reading a book.

The doorbell rang,

but when she opened the door,

no one was there.

"Who rang?" she shouted.

"What's this old sack doing here?"
Pearl reached into the sack
and pulled out the apples
and nuts and berries.

"Oh, boy, look at these!"

she said to herself.

"I can make pies!"

Then Pearl pulled out

the pink and blue stones

and the red leaves.

"Oh, swell! Look at these!"

she said to herself.

Then Pearl reached further

into the sack—

and she screamed, "Eek!"

Peewee jumped out of the sack.

He had purple clover all over him.

The others came out of the bushes.

"Here we are!" shouted Peewee.

"All your favorite things!

Happy birthday, sweetheart!"

GHOSTS

Often when it snowed in the winter,
Mo and his friends
went to Aunt Minnie's.

They sat by the fire
and played cards.
They drank hot chocolate
and told stories to each other.

One night Peewee told

a very scary story

about a ghost.

When he finished, the animals heard
a creaking noise in the hall.
"Oh, dear! A ghost!"
cried Aunt Minnie.

"No, no, Aunt Minnie," said Sheriff Mo.

"Ghosts aren't real.

It's only the old wood singing a song."

Suddenly the curtain moved
and a strange sound
came from the window.

"Eek!" cried Pearl. "A ghost!"

"No, no, Pearl," said Mo.

"Ghosts aren't real.

It's only the wind saying hello."

Then scratching sounds
came from the wall.
"Sheriff!" cried Peewee.
"It's a ghost!"
"No, no, Peewee," said Mo.
"It's only a little mouse in the wall
trying to keep warm."

"Oh, Sheriff!" cried Chicken Lucille.

"I hear breathing sounds!

It's a ghost!"

"Lucille, Lucille, don't fret,"

said Mo. "It's only the daylight

sleeping and dreaming."

All the animals were very quiet

as they listened to the sounds

of the wood and the north wind

and the mouse and the daylight.

Suddenly a picture fell off the wall
behind Sheriff Mo.

Mo leaped out of his chair.

"A *ghost!*"

"Sheriff, Sheriff, it's only
a picture falling!" the animals cried.
"Goodness, goodness!" said Mo,
holding his heart.

All the animals laughed at Mo.

The sheriff himself laughed hardest.

"Let's toast good friends!" he said.

"Hear, hear!" everyone cheered.